The Sword in the Stove

To Emily, the yin to my yang

ATHENEUM BOOKS FOR YOUNG READERS
An imprint of Simon & Schuster Children's Publishing Division
1230 Avenue of the Americas, New York, New York 10020
Copyright © 2016 by Frank W. Dormer
All rights reserved, including the right of reproduction in whole or in part in any form.
ATHENEUM BOOKS FOR YOUNG READERS is a registered trademark of Simon & Schuster, Inc.
Atheneum logo is a trademark of Simon & Schuster, Inc.
For information about special discounts for bulk purchases, please contact Simon & Schuster Special Sales at 1-866-506-1949 or business@simonandschuster.com.
The Simon & Schuster Speakers Bureau can bring authors to your live event. For more information or to book an event, contact the Simon & Schuster Speakers Bureau at 1-866-248-3049 or visit our website at www.simonspeakers.com.
Book design by Sonia Chaghatzbanian
The text for this book is set in Chipperfield_and_Bailey, Aged, and Sattler AS.
The illustrations for this book are rendered in watercolors.
Manufactured in China
0216 SCP
First Edition
10 9 8 7 6 5 4 3 2 1
Library of Congress Cataloging-in-Publication Data
Dormer, Frank W., author, illustrator.
The sword in the stove / Frank W. Dormer. — First edition.
pages cm
ISBN 978-1-4814-3167-5 (hardcover)
ISBN 978-1-4814-3168-2 (eBook)
[1. Missing persons—Fiction. 2. Knights and knighthood—Fiction. 3. Imagination—Fiction. 4. Humorous stories.]
I. Title.
PZ7.D7283Swo 2016
[E]—dc23   2014035209

Gotta go, gotta go, gotta go

THE Sword IN THE Stove

Story and pictures by FRANK W. DORMER

otta go, gotta go . . .

Atheneum Books for Young Readers   New York   London   Toronto   Sydney   New Delhi

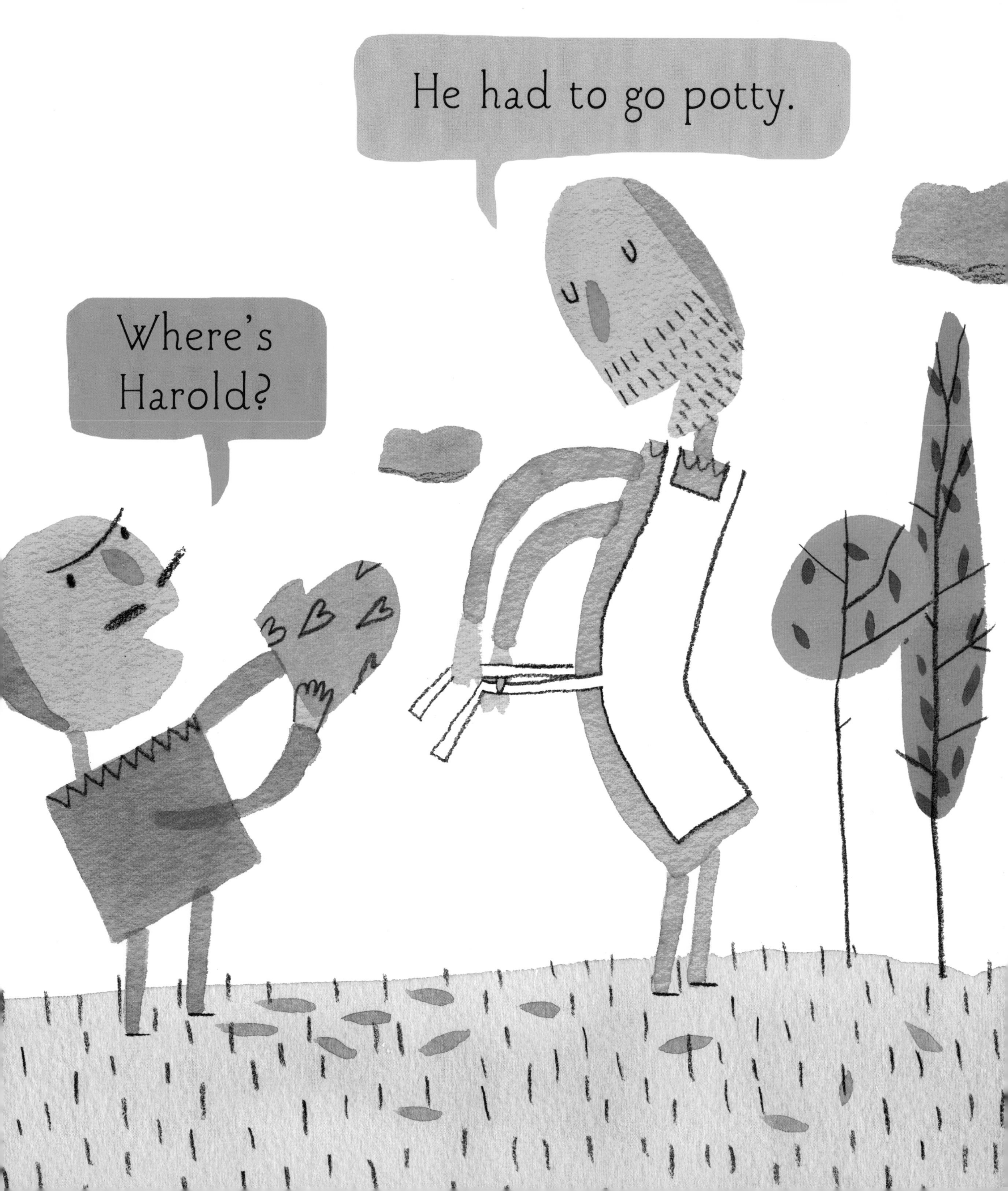
He had to go potty.
Where's Harold?

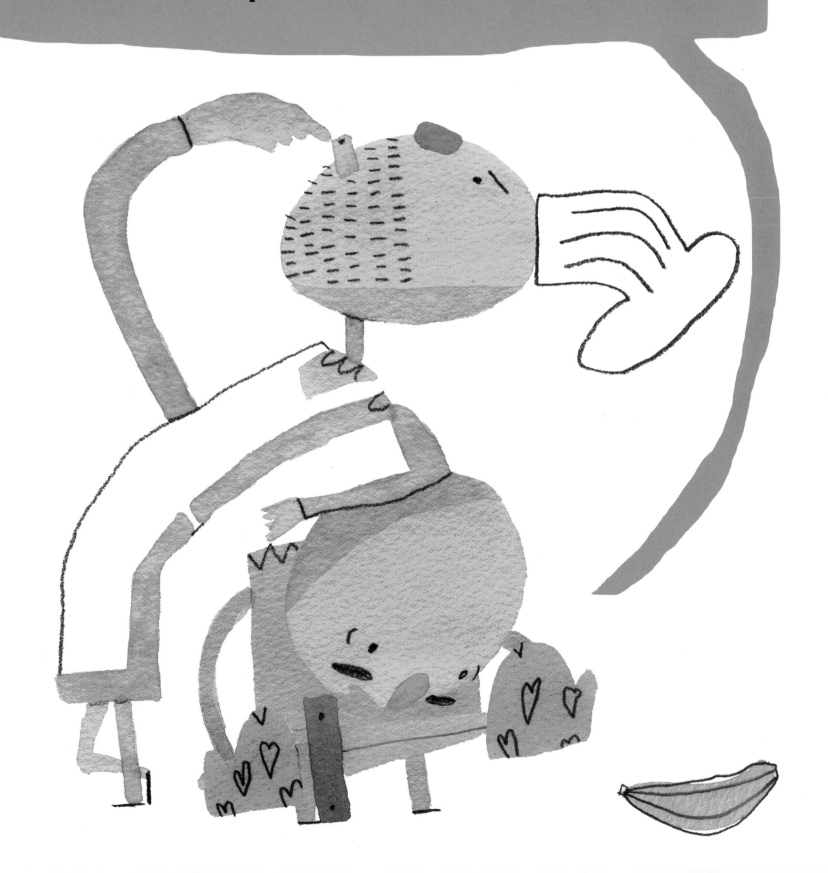

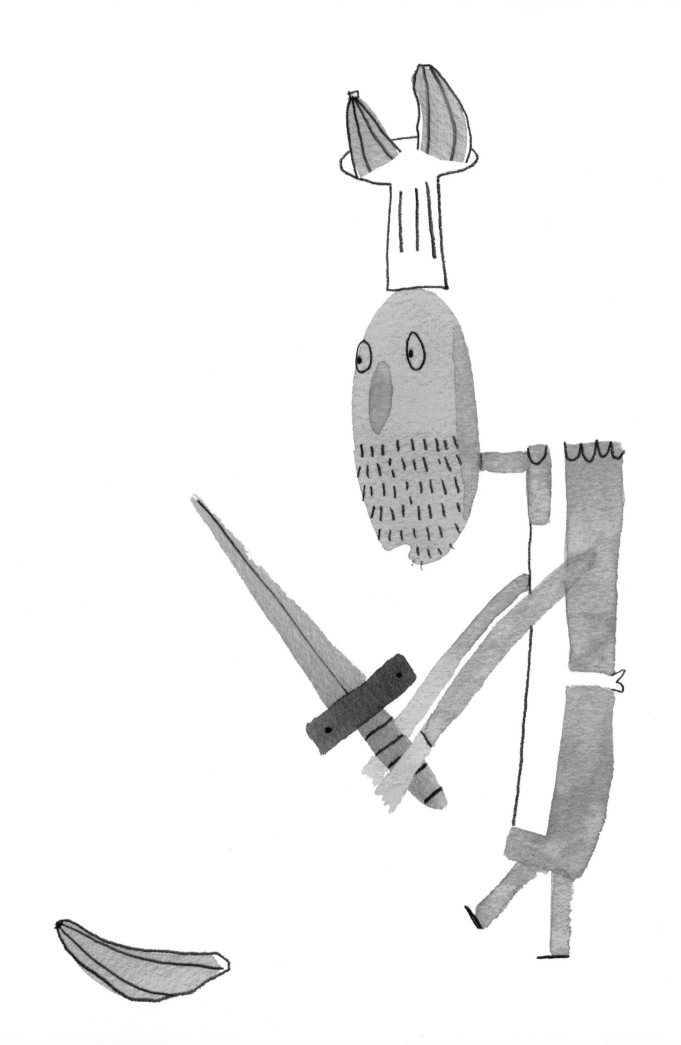

VIKINGS!

Who will steal our cookies and make us say . . .

I would.